DUCK and SPIDER

WRITTEN AND ILLUSTRATED BY

Barbara Jean Nagle

DUCK and SPIDER

Written by: Barbara Jean Nagle
Illustrated by: Barbara Jean Nagle

This book for Zoe Jean Kingsley in memory
of her mother and my daughter
Lisa Jean Kelly

THE STORY OF
DUCK AND SPIDER

 After a long cold winter, it was finally springtime, and Mother Duck was getting ready to lay her spring eggs. "I must find the best spot in the farmyard," thought Mother Duck. "I want my babies to have a safe, warm and dry nest."

Mother Duck looked and looked everywhere in the old farmyard, but nothing seemed just right.

At last she found the perfect spot next to the old moss covered stonewall and the beautiful tall orange lilies. Mother Duck then made a splendid nest, warm and cozy and filled with only the best straw she could find. Then Mother Duck proceeded to sit and lay her eggs.

As she was sitting, keeping her eggs warm, Mother Duck noticed a web in the stonewall.

When Mother Duck looked closer she saw a lovely black and yellow spider with golden eyes looking right back at her! "Hi, Spider," said Mother Duck. "Have you been there a long time?"

"Yes," said the Spider, "I've watched you for days, from the moment that you were walking all over the farmyard, here and there. I thought you were crazy, and then I watched you build your nest right next to mine."

"Oh, yes," replied Mother Duck, "and haven't I just made a grand nest?"

"I'm not too sure," said the Spider. "Reddy the Fox comes this way everyday and jumps over the wall just about where you are sitting."

"Well, he'll just have to jump somewhere else. This is my nest and I'm not moving," said Mother Duck rather sternly.

"Oh well, do what you want, but I understand that a fox will eat duck eggs. You better be careful," warned the Spider.

Well, that night Mother Duck went soundly to sleep. She was exhausted from all her hard work from finding a nest, making the nest, laying her eggs, and her long talk with Spider. "But that was rather nice she thought, to have a friend nearby, even if it was a spider."

Then just around midnight, over the stonewall jumped Reddy the Fox, right on top of Mother Duck's head!

"Quack! Quack! Quack!" screamed Mother Duck. "What are you doing, you bad, bad, bad fox? Don't you look before you jump?"

"Oh, I'm so sorry," said the fox, all out of breath. Now, this was a very smart fox, he saw all the great big duck eggs, and so he said with a sneaky smile: "I'll jump somewhere else from now on. You don't need to worry, Mother Duck." And off ran Reddy the Fox.

Spider, who was startled awake by all the noise, said, " See? I told you the fox jumped over this wall right where you are sitting, but you didn't listen."

"He won't come back," said Mother Duck.

Well the next night, Mother Duck went to sleep. In the morning when she counted her eggs, one was missing!

"Quack! Quack! Quack! Wake up, Spider. Do you have my egg?" Mother Duck frantically wanted to know.

"You silly duck," replied Spider, "what would I do with your egg, and for heaven's sake, where would I hide it? Reddy the Fox probably took your egg and is eating it for breakfast right this very moment!"

"Oh, my! We must not let this happen again. This is terrible," said sad Mother Duck. So Mother Duck and Spider thought and thought for a very long time. "I know," said the Spider, "we'll take turns staying awake in the nighttime to guard your nest."

That night, Spider guarded the nest while
Mother Duck slept. Then Spider would wake up
Mother Duck, and it would be Mother Duck's
turn to guard the nest. This worked just great,
until Spider and Mother Duck both fell asleep at

the same time, and at that very moment, Reddy the Fox ran off with another juicy egg!
In the morning Mother Duck counted her eggs. "Quack! Quack! Quack!" cried Mother Duck. "Another egg is missing. This is horrible. Our plan didn't work. What should we do?" fretted mother duck.

We'll have to think of another
Plan," said Spider. After a long time of thinking,
Spider finally said, "I have an idea, we'll just
have to move your nest to the other end of the

stonewall so that Reddy the Fox won't know where we are."

So Mother Duck and Spider moved all the eggs down to the other end of the stonewall. Spider spun a new web right next to Mother Duck. Then both Mother Duck and Spider fell sound asleep right after dinner.

Well, that night, Reddy the Fox showed up at the old nest. "Now, where is that duck and her delicious eggs," thought the sneaky fox. "I'll just have to use my talented nose and find them."

So Reddy the Fox started sniffing the ground and followed his nose, and it led him right to the other end of the stone wall, exactly where Mother Duck was now sitting soundly asleep!

"Yum, Yum, Yum," thought the fox as he trotted off with another big juicy egg.

In the morning, Mother Duck woke up, and then she counted her eggs.

"Quack! Quackkkk! Quackkk! One of my precious eggs is gone! What am I going to do" Soon all my eggs will be gone. Then I won't have any babies," complained Mother Duck. Mother Duck felt really bad because their plan did not work. Spider did not want to see Mother Duck sad, so Spider thought and thought for a very long time, as Mother Duck was gloomily sitting on her nest with her head hanging down.

"I've got it," whooped the Spider. "At last, this is the best idea in the world. I promise this will work. I'm a spider, and I should have thought of this idea in the first place, how silly!" Mother Duck could not wait to hear of the spider's grand idea.

"Listen," said the Spider, "each night when you go to sleep, I will spin a giant web around you. Then when Reddy the Fox touches the web, I will feel it vibrate, which will in turn wake me up, you know, just like when I'm catching bugs to eat, except this time it will be a really big bug! We'll have to change Reddy the Foxes name to Reddy the Bug," laughed the Spider. "I'll wake you up when the web shakes. What do you think of the idea, Mother Duck?" "It sounds like an extraordinary idea," said a very happy Mother Duck. "I hope it works." "Don't worry," said Spider, "my web always works." So that very night, as Mother Duck settled down to sleep, Spider spun a web around her nest. It was Fantastic! It was the biggest web the spider had ever made!

Then late that night, when Mother Duck and
Spider were sleeping, up crept Reddy the Fox.
Well, he didn't see or smell that web around
Mother Duck, and when he stuck his nose into
her nest, it was too late! Reddy the Fox was all
tangled up, just like a big bug! Spider woke up
and yelled, "wake up! wake up! wake up!"

Mother Duck woke up with a start. "Quack! Quack! Quack!
"What is the matter?" she wanted to know.
"We caught the fox, you silly duck! Said the proud spider. "Oh please let me go. I promise never to eat another egg," pleaded the fox. "Oh please, don't eat me, spider, let me go, Please!"

"After all those eggs you ate, you should be nice and fat by now, and you'd make a good breakfast for me, except you are too big and have too much fur for my taste," said the spider. "But if you ever eat another one of Mother Duck's eggs, I will call all my spider friends and we'll make a feast of you, fur and all!"

"I promise never to eat another one of Mother Duck's eggs," said the fox, shaking like a leaf because he was so scared.

Mother Duck and Spider untangled Reddy the Fox and watched him run to the woods as fast as the wind!

"Well, we fixed him good," said the spider.
"Let's move back to the old nest by the beautiful
orange lilies."

So Mother Duck and Spider rolled
all the big duck eggs back to the old nest and
were very tired, but just before they went to
sleep, Mother Duck counted her eggs to be sure
they didn't leave any behind.

"Ten eggs, that means I'll have ten babies any day now. How wonderful," thought Mother Duck. Then she fell asleep dreaming about cute little fuzzy baby ducks.

In the morning, Mother Duck checked her eggs. None had hatched yet, but wait, she counted only nine eggs!

She counted them again to be sure. "ONLY NINE EGGS! QUACK! QUACK! QUACK! OH, QUACK! "

Mother Duck and Spider were shocked. Reddy the Fox had taken another egg, how terrible. He broke his promise. "I just don't know what to think," said Spider. "What are we to do now?" said Mother Duck.

"But wait, what is that way over near the well? It looks, IT LOOKS LIKE YOUR MISSING EGG!" yelled the spider, jumping for joy, making his web act like a trampoline.

Mother Duck practically flew to the well. It was her egg! They could not figure out how in the world the egg got near the well.

In a few days, Mother Duck's eggs hatched into beautiful little fluffy yellow ducklings. Mother Duck and Spider were over joyed!

As the ducklings grew, Spider told them the
tales of the terrible sneaky fox, and warned them
to be careful when they became parents.
"Always have a spider friend to protect you,"
Spider recommended.

Reddy the Fox, well he continued to be a pest to all the farm animals, sneaking around, scaring the chickens, getting chased by the farm dog. But because of his promise, he always left Mother Duck and her babies alone. Also, he did not think being breakfast for Spider and his friends would be much fun, so he stayed away from Spider too. But for some reason, every time he walked by Mother duck and Spider, he could hardly keep himself from laughing out loud. So he just walked by with that sneaky little grin on his face. Do you know why? What do you think?

Well, you know I think Reddy the Fox thought it was a big joke the morning he grabbed one of Mother Duck's eggs and hid it near the well. He did not eat it, just as he promised, but you know that fox just had to have some fun!

THE END

Mother Duck is out to find the most perfect place to raise her baby ducklings when they hatch. But what Mother Duck does not know is that she is about to make a new friend, and together they will outsmart the sneaky fox that lives nearby. This story will help teach children the value of friendship, loyalty, heroism, morals and the care and trust of a true friend. Children the world over will relate to this delightful story of Mother Duck and Spider.

Barbara Jean Nagle grew up in Massachusetts surrounded with all kinds of animals. "We had chickens, dogs, cats, pigs, goats, horses, birds and ducks. My father would tell me stories that he made up all the time, and I loved to sit on his knee and hear them all. When I had my own children I would often sit and tell them stories that I made up. One day I decided to write them down and I hope you liked this one about Mother Duck and Spider."

Books by Barbara Nagle that I am sure you will enjoy.

Duck and Spider
Tabitha
The Tabitha Tree
Secret Friends
Henry and Sara
Change the World Cookbook
Skye
Dinner at Dragon's House

I would love to hear from you with your comments or questions.
You may contact me by email:
Zling13@comcast.net

Made in the USA
Middletown, DE
10 December 2021

55075185R00022